BABY RHINO'S ESCAPE

JPB
K

Copyright © 1992 by Adrienne Kennaway

The moral right of the author has been asserted

First published in Great Britain in 1992 by Hamish Hamilton Ltd

This edition first published in 1997 by Happy Cat Books,
Bradfield, Essex CO11 2UT

A CIP catalogue record for this book is available from the British Library

ISBN 1 899248 51 X

Printed in China by Imago

BABY RHINO'S ESCAPE

ADRIENNE KENNAWAY

Happy Cat Books

Deep in the heart of Africa, Rhino lived with
his mother. Rhino was only a baby.
He had a lot to learn.

"Why is there a bird on my head?" asked Rhino. "That's Egret, our friend," answered his mother. "She pecks juicy insects off our rough skin."

"Look! There's a lion!" Rhino said.

"Don't be afraid," said his mother. "We can charge him."
And they did.

Charging was fun! Rhino
charged everything he
could see on the grassland
plains, even little thorn trees.

"Watch me!" shouted Rhino,
and charged the antelopes.
They ran off in all directions.

Rhino felt very brave. He charged the giraffe.
"Don't go too close," warned his mother.

One day storm clouds darkened the
sky and the dry season ended.
A flash of lightning set the dry grass alight.

Tongues of flame swept across the plains.
"Fire, fire!" Egret flapped her wings to
warn her friends.

In the stampede for the river, Rhino lost his mother.
"Where are you?" he called.

Rhino and the other animals jumped into the river and paddled hard for the other side. They knew that fire wouldn't follow them across the water.

It started to rain. Big heavy drops fell in Rhino's eyes.
He didn't see Crocodile coming nearer and nearer…

But Egret did. She swooped down
from the sky to save her friend.

Crocodile snapped his great jaws and sank slowly back into the river. Rhino squelched up the muddy slope as fast as he could. "Thank you, Egret," he panted.

Rhino's mother was on the riverbank. She was overjoyed
to see Rhino again. Together they looked at the burnt,
black grass. "Fire is danger," said Rhino's mother.

Later Egret flew down to join her friends.
Now they were all safe together again.

9/00